ONCE A GREECH

ONCE A GREECH

by Evelyn E. Smith

The mildest of men, Iversen was capable of murder . . . to disprove Harkaway's hypothesis that in the midst of life, we are in life!

Just two weeks before the S. S. *Herringbone* of the Interstellar Exploration, Examination (and Exploitation) Service was due to start her return journey to Earth, one of her scouts disconcertingly reported the discovery of intelligent life in the Virago System.

"Thirteen planets," Captain Iversen snarled, wishing there were someone on whom he could place the blame for this mischance, "and we spend a full year here exploring each one of them with all the resources of Terrestrial science and technology, and what happens? On the nineteenth moon of the eleventh planet, intelligent life is discovered. And who has to discover it? Harkaway, of all people. I thought for sure all the moons were cinders or I would never have sent him out to them just to keep him from getting in my hair."

"The boy's not a bad boy, sir," the first officer said. "Just a thought incompetent, that's all—which is to be expected if the Service will choose its officers on the basis of written examinations. I'm glad to see him make good."

Iversen would have been glad to see Harkaway make good, too, only such a concept seemed utterly beyond the bounds of possibility. From the moment the young man had first set foot on the S. S. *Herringbone*, he had seemed unable to make anything but bad. Even in such a conglomeration of fools under Captain Iverson, his idiocy was of outstanding quality.

The captain, however, had not been wholly beyond reproach in this instance, as he himself knew. Pity he had made such an error about the eleventh planet's moons. It was really such a small mistake.

ONCE A GREECH

Moons one to eighteen and twenty to forty-six still appeared to be cinders. It was all too easy for the spectroscope to overlook Flimbot, the nineteenth.

But it would be Flimbot which had turned out to be a green and pleasant planet, very similar to Earth. Or so Harkaway reported on the intercom.

"And the other forty-five aren't really moons at all," he began. "They're—"

"You can tell me all that when we reach Flimbot," Iversen interrupted, "which should be in about six hours. Remember, that intercom uses a lot of power and we're tight on fuel."

But it proved to be more than six *days* later before the ship reached Flimbot. This was owing to certain mechanical difficulties that arose when the crew tried to lift the mother ship from the third planet, on which it was based. For sentimental reasons, the IEE(E) always tried to establish its prime base on the third planet of a system. Anyhow, when the *Herringbone* was on the point of takeoff, it was discovered that the rock-eating species which was the only life on the third planet had eaten all the projecting metal parts on the ship, including the rocket-exhaust tubes, the airlock handles and the chromium trim.

"I had been wondering what made the little fellows so sick," Smullyan, the ship's doctor, said. "They went wump, wump, wump all night long, until my heart bled for them. Ah, everywhere it goes, humanity spreads the fell seeds of death and destruction—"

"Are you a doctor or a veterinarian?" Iversen demanded furiously. "By Betelgeuse, you act as if I'd crammed those blasted tubes down their stinking little throats!"

"It was you who invaded their paradise with your ship. It was you—"

"Shut up!" Iversen yelled. "Shut up, shut up, shut up, shut up!"

6

So Dr. Smullyan went off, like many a ship's physician before him, and got good and drunk on the medical stores.

*

By the time they finally arrived on Flimbot, Harkaway had already gone native. He appeared at the airlock wearing nothing but a brief, colorful loincloth of alien fabric and a wreath of flowers in his hair. He was fondling a large, woolly pink caterpillar.

"Where is your uniform, sir!" Captain Iversen barked, aghast. If there was one thing he was intolerant of in his command, it was sloppiness.

"This is the undress uniform of the Royal Flimbotzi Navy, sir. I was given the privilege of wearing one as a great *msu'gri*—honor—to our race. If I were to return to my own uniform, it might set back diplomatic relations between Flimbot and Earth as much as—"

"All right!" the captain snapped. "All right, all right, all right!"

He didn't ask any questions about the Royal Flimbotzi Navy. He had deduced its nature when, on nearing Flimbot, he had discovered that the eleventh planet actually had only one moon. The other forty-five celestial objects were spacecraft, quaint and primitive, it was true, but spacecraft nonetheless. Probably it was their orbital formation that had made him think they were moons. Oh, the crew must be in great spirits; they did so enjoy having a good laugh at his expense!

He looked for something with which to reproach Harkaway, and his eye lighted on the caterpillar. "What's that thing you're carrying there?" he barked.

Raising itself on its tail, the caterpillar barked right back at him.

Captain Iversen paled. First he had overlooked the spacecraft, and now, after thirty years of faithful service to the IEE(E) in the less desirable sectors of space, he had committed the ultimate error in his first contact with a new form of intelligent life!

"Sorry, sir," he said, forgetting that the creature—whatever its mental prowess—could hardly be expected to understand Terran yet. "I am just a simple spaceman and my ways are crude, but I mean no harm." He whirled on Harkaway. "I thought you said the natives were humanoid."

The young officer grinned. "They are. This is just a greech. Cuddly little fellow, isn't he?" The greech licked Harkaway's face with a tripartite blue tongue. "The Flimbotzik are mad about pets. Great animal-lovers. That's how I knew I could trust them right from the start. Show me a life-form that loves animals, I always say, and—"

"I'm not interested in what you always say," Iversen interrupted, knowing Harkaway's premise was fundamentally unsound, because he himself was the kindliest of all men, and he hated animals. And, although he didn't hate Harkaway, who was not an animal, save in the strictly Darwinian sense, he could not repress unsportsmanlike feelings of bitterness.

Why couldn't it have been one of the other officers who had discovered the Flimbotzik? Why must it be Harkaway—the most inept of his scouts, whose only talent seemed to be the egregious error, who always rushed into a thing half-cocked, who mistook superficialities for profundities, Harkaway, the blundering fool, the blithering idiot—who had stumbled into this greatest discovery of Iversen's career? And, of course, Harkaway's, too. Well, life was like that and always had been.

"Have you tested those air and soil samples yet?" Iversen snarled into his communicator, for his spacesuit was beginning to itch again as the gentle warmth of Flimbot activated certain small and opportunistic life-forms which had emigrated from a previous system along with the Terrans.

"We're running them through as fast as we can, sir," said a harried voice. "We can offer you no more than our poor best."

"But why bother with all that?" Harkaway wanted to know. "This planet is absolutely safe for human life. I can guarantee it personally."

"On what basis?" Iversen asked.

"Well, I've been here two weeks and I've survived, haven't I?"

"That," Iversen told him, "does not prove that the planet can sustain human life."

Harkaway laughed richly. "Wonderful how you can still keep that marvelous sense of humor, Skipper, after all the things that have been going wrong on the voyage. Ah, here comes the *flim'tuu*—the welcoming committee," he said quickly. "They were a little shy before. Because of the rockets, you know."

"Don't their ships have any?"

"They don't seem to. They're really very primitive affairs, barely able to go from planet to planet."

"If they *go*," Iversen said, "stands to reason *something* must power them."

"I really don't know what it is," Harkaway retorted defensively. "After all, even though I've been busy as a beaver, three weeks would hardly give me time to investigate every aspect of their culture. . . . Don't you think the natives are remarkably humanoid?" he changed the subject.

They were, indeed. Except for a somewhat greenish cast of countenance and distinctly purple hair, as they approached, in their brief, gay garments and flower garlands, the natives resembled nothing so much as a group of idealized South Sea Islanders of the nineteenth century.

Gigantic butterflies whizzed about their heads. Countless small animals frisked about their feet—more of the pink caterpillars; bright blue creatures that were a winsome combination of monkey and koala; a kind of large, merry-eyed snake that moved by holding its tail in its mouth and rolling like a hoop. All had faces that reminded the captain of the work of the celebrated twentieth-century artist W. Disney.

"By Polaris," he cried in disgust, "I might have known you'd find a *cute* planet!"

"Moon, actually," the first officer said, "since it is in orbit around Virago XI, rather than Virago itself."

"Would you have *wanted* them to be hostile?" Harkaway asked peevishly. "Honestly, some people never seem to be satisfied."

From his proprietary airs, one would think Harkaway had created the natives himself. "At least, with hostile races, you know where you are," Iversen said. "I always suspect friendly life-forms. Friendliness simply isn't a natural instinct."

"Who's being anthropomorphic now!" Harkaway chided.

Iversen flushed, for he had berated the young man for that particular fault on more than one occasion. Harkaway was too prone to interpret alien traits in terms of terrestrial culture. Previously, since all intelligent life-forms with which the *Herringbone* had come into contact had already been discovered by somebody else, that didn't matter too much. In this instance, however, any mistakes of contact or interpretation mattered terribly. And Iversen couldn't see Harkaway not making a mistake; the boy simply didn't have it in him.

"You know you're superimposing our attitude on theirs," the junior officer continued tactlessly. "The Flimbotzik are a simple, friendly, *shig-livi* people, closely resembling some of our historical primitives—in a nice way, of course."

"None of our primitives had space travel," Iversen pointed out.

"Well, you couldn't really call those things spaceships," Harkaway said deprecatingly.

"They go through space, don't they? I don't know what else you'd call them."

"One judges the primitiveness of a race by its cultural and technological institutions," Harkaway said, with a lofty smile. "And these people are laughably backward. Why, they even believe in reincarnation—*mpoola*, they call it."

"How do you know all this?" Iversen demanded. "Don't tell me you profess to speak the language already?"

"It's not a difficult language," Harkaway said modestly, "and I have managed to pick up quite a comprehensive smattering. I dare-say I haven't caught all the nuances—*heeka lob peeka*, as the Flimbotzik themselves say—but they are a very simple people and probably they don't have—"

"Are we going to keep them waiting," Iversen asked, "while we discuss nuances? Since you say you speak the language so well, suppose you make them a pretty speech all about how the Earth government extends the—I suppose it would be hand, in this instance—of friendship to Flimbot and—"

Harkaway blushed. "I sort of did that already, acting as your deputy. *Mpoo*—status—means so much in these simple societies, you know, and they seemed to expect something of the sort. However, I'll introduce you to the Flimflim—the king, you know—" he pointed to an imposing individual in the forefront of the crowd—"and get over all the amenities, shall I?"

"It would be jolly good of you," Iversen said frigidly.

*

It was a pity they hadn't discovered Flimbot much earlier in their survey of the Virago System, Iversen thought with regret, because it

11

was truly a pleasant spot and a week was very little time in which to explore a world and study a race, even one as simple as the gentle Flimbotzik actually turned out to be. It seemed amazing that they should have developed anything as advanced as space travel, when their only ground conveyances were a species of wagon drawn by plookik, a species of animal.

But Iversen had no time for further investigation. The *Herringbone's* fuel supply was calculated almost to the minute and so, willy-nilly, the Earthmen had to leave beautiful Flimbot at the end of the week, knowing little more about the Flimbotzik than they had before they came. Only Harkaway, who had spent the three previous weeks on Flimbot, had any further knowledge of the Flimbotzik—and Iversen had little faith in any data he might have collected.

"I don't believe Harkaway knows the language nearly as well as he pretends to," Iversen told the first officer as both of them watched the young lieutenant make the formal speech of farewell.

"Come now," the first officer protested. "Seems to me the boy is doing quite well. Acquired a remarkable command of the language, considering he's been here only four weeks."

"Remarkable, I'll grant you, but is it accurate?"

"He seems to communicate and that is the ultimate objective of language, is it not?"

"Then why did the Flimbotzik fill the tanks with wine when I distinctly told him to ask for water?"

Of course the ship could synthesize water from its own waste products, if necessary, but there was no point in resorting to that expedient when a plentiful supply of pure H_2O was available on the world.

"A very understandable error, sir. Harkaway explained it to me. It seems the word for water, *m'koog*, is very similar to the word for wine, *mk'oog*. Harkaway himself admits his pronunciation isn't perfect and—"

"All right," Iversen interrupted. "What I'd like to know is what happened to the *mk'oog*, then—"

"The *m'koog*, you mean? It's in the tanks."

"—because, when they came to drain the wine out of the tanks to put the water in, the tanks were already totally empty."

"I have no idea," the first officer said frostily, "no idea at all. If you'll glance at my papers, you'll note I'm Temperance by affiliation, but if you'd like to search my cabin, anyway, I—"

"By Miaplacidus, man," Iversen exclaimed, "I wasn't accusing you! Of that, anyway!"

Everybody on the vessel was so confoundedly touchy. Lucky they had a stable commanding officer like himself, or morale would simply go to pot.

*

"Well, it's all over," Harkaway said, joining them up at the airlock in one lithe bound—a mean feat in that light gravity. "And a right good speech, if I do say so myself. The Flimflim says he will count the thlubbzik with ardent expectation until the mission from Earth arrives with the promised gifts."

"Just what gifts did you take it upon yourself to—" Iversen began, when he was interrupted by a voice behind them crying, "Woe, woe, woe!"

And, thrusting himself past the three other officers, Dr. Smullyan addressed the flim'puu, or farewell committee, assembled outside the ship. "Do not let the Earthmen return to your fair planet, O happily ignorant Flimbotzik," he declaimed, "lest wretchedness and misery be your lot as a result. Tell them, 'Hence!' Tell them, 'Begone!' Tell

13

them, 'Avaunt!' For, know ye, humanity is a blight, a creeping canker—"

He was interrupted by the captain's broad palm clamping down over his mouth.

"Clap him in the brig, somebody, until we get clear of this place," Iversen ordered wearily. "If Harkaway could pick up the Flimbotzi language, the odds are that some of the natives have picked up Terran."

"That's right, always keep belittling me," Harkaway said sulkily as two of the crewmen carried off the struggling medical officer, who left an aromatic wake behind him that bore pungent testimonial to where a part, at least, of the *mk'oog* had gone. "No wonder it took me so long to find myself."

"Oh, have you found yourself at last?" Iversen purred. "Splendid! Now that you know where you are, supposing you do me a big favor and go lose yourself again while we make ready for blastoff."

"For shame," said the first officer as Harkaway stamped off. "For shame!"

"The captain's a hard man," observed the chief petty officer, who was lounging negligently against a wall, doing nothing.

"Ay, that he is," agreed the crewman who was assisting him. "That he is—a hard man, indeed."

"By Caroli, be quiet, all of you!" Iversen yelled. The very next voyage, he was going to have a new crew if he had to transfer to Colonization to do it! Even colonists couldn't be as obnoxious as the sons of space with which he was cursed.

*

It was only after the *Herringbone* had left the Virago System entirely that Iversen discovered Harkaway had taken the greech along.

"But you can't abscond with one of the natives' pets!" he protested, overlooking, for the sake of rhetoric, the undeniable fact that Harkaway had already done so and that there could be no turning back. It would expend too much precious fuel and leave them stranded for life on Virago XI^a.

"Nonsense, sir!" Harkaway retorted. "Didn't the Flimflim say everything on Flimbot was mine? *Thlu'pt shig-nliv, snusnigg bnig-nliv* were his very words. Anyhow, they have plenty more greechi. They won't miss this little one."

"But he may have belonged to someone," Iversen objected. "An incident like this could start a war."

"I don't see how he could have belonged to anyone. Followed me around most of the time I was there. We've become great pals, haven't we, little fellow?" He ruffled the greech's pink fur and the creature gave a delighted squeal.

Iversen could already see that the greechik were going to be Flimbot's first lucrative export. From time immemorial, the people of Earth had been susceptible to cuddly little life-forms, which was why Earth had nearly been conquered by the zz^{iu} from Sirius VII, before they discovered them to be hostile and quite intelligent life-forms rather than a new species of tabby.

"Couldn't bear to leave him," Harkaway went on as the greech draped itself around his shoulders and regarded Iversen with large round blue eyes. "The Flimflim won't mind, because I promised him an elephant."

"You mean the diplomatic mission will have to waste valuable cargo space on an *elephant*!" Iversen sputtered. "And you should know, if anyone does, just how spacesick an elephant can get. By Pherkad, Lieutenant Harkaway, you had no authority to make any promises to the Flimflim!"

ONCE A GREECH

"I discovered the Flimbotzik," Harkaway said sullenly. "*I* learned the language. *I* established rapport. Just because you happen to be the commander of this expedition doesn't mean you're God, Captain Iversen!"

"Harkaway," the captain barked, "this smacks of downright mutiny! Go to your cabin forthwith and memorize six verses of the Spaceman's Credo!"

The greech lifted its head and barked back at Iversen, again. "That's my brave little watch-greech," Harkaway said fondly. "As a matter of fact, sir," he told the captain, "that was just what I was proposing to do myself. Go to my cabin, I mean; I have no time to waste on inferior prose. I plan to spend the rest of the voyage, or such part as I can spare from my duties—"

"You're relieved of them," Iversen said grimly.

"—working on my book. It's all about the doctrine of *mpoola*—reincarnation, or, if you prefer, metempsychosis. The Flimbotzi religion is so similar to many of the earlier terrestrial theologies—Hindu, Greek, Egyptian, Southern Californian—that sometimes one is almost tempted to stop and wonder if simplicity is not the essence of truth."

Iversen knew that, for the sake of discipline, he should not, once he had ordered Harkaway to his cabin, stop to bandy words, but he was a chronic word-bandier, having inherited the trait from his stalwart Viking ancestors. "How can you have learned all about their religion, their doctrine of reincarnation, in just four ridiculously short weeks?"

"It's a gift," Harkaway said modestly.

"Go to your cabin, sir! No, wait a moment!" For, suddenly overcome by a strange, warm, utterly repulsive emotion, Iversen pointed a quivering finger at the caterpillar. "Did you bring along the proper food for that—that thing? Can't have him starving, you know," he added gruffly. After all, he was a humane man, he told himself; it wasn't that he found the creature tugging at his heart-strings, or anything like that.

"Oh, he'll eat anything we eat, sir. As long as it's not meat. All the species on Flimbot are herbivores. I can't figure out whether the Flimbotzik themselves are vegetarians because they practice *mpoola*, or practice *mpoola* because they're—"

"I don't want to hear another word about *mpoola* or about Flimbot!" Iversen yelled. "Get out of here! And stay away from the library!"

"I have already exhausted its painfully limited resources, sir." Harkaway saluted with grace and withdrew to his cabin, wearing the greech like an affectionate lei about his neck.

*

Iverson heard no more about *mpoola* from Harkaway—who, though he did not remain confined to his cabin when he had pursuits to pursue in other parts of the ship, at least had the tact to keep out of the captain's way as much as possible—but the rest of his men seemed able to talk of nothing else. The voyage back from a star system was always longer in relative terms than the voyage out, because the thrill of new worlds to explore was gone; already anticipating boredom, the men were ripe for almost any distraction.

On one return voyage, the whole crew had set itself to the study of Hittite with very creditable results. On another, they had all devoted themselves to the ancient art of alchemy, and, after nearly blowing up the ship, had come up with an elixir which, although not the quintessence—as they had, in their initial enthusiasm, alleged—proved to be an effective cure for hiccups. Patented under the name of Herringbone Hiccup Shoo, it brought each one of them an income which would have been enough to support them in more than modest comfort for the rest of their lives.

However, the adventurous life seemed to exert an irresistible lure upon them and they all shipped upon the *Herringbone* again—much to the captain's dismay, for he had hoped for a fresh start with a new crew and there seemed to be no way of getting rid of them short of reaching retirement age.

The men weren't quite ready to accept *mpoola* as a practical religion—Harkaway hadn't finished his book yet—but as something very close to it. The concept of reincarnation had always been very appealing to the human mind, which would rather have envisaged itself perpetuated in the body of a cockroach than vanishing completely into nothingness.

"It's all so logical, sir," the first officer told Iversen. "The individuality or the soul or the psyche—however you want to look at it—starts the essentially simple cycle of life as a greech—"

"Why as a greech?" Iversen asked, humoring him for the moment. "There are lower life-forms on Flimbot."

"I don't know." The first officer sounded almost testy. "That's where Harkaway starts the progression."

"Harkaway! Is there no escaping that cretin's name?"

"Sir," said the first officer, "may I speak frankly?"

"No," Iversen said, "you may not."

"Your skepticism arises less from disbelief than from the fact that you are jealous of Harkaway because it was he who made the great discovery, not you."

"Which great discovery?" Iversen asked, sneering to conceal his hurt at being so overwhelmingly misunderstood. "Flimbot or *mpoola?*"

"Both," the first officer said. "You refuse to accept the fact that this hitherto incompetent youth has at last blossomed forth in the lambent colors of genius, just as the worthy greech becomes a zkoort, and the clean-living zkoort in his turn passes on to the next higher plane of existence, which is, in the Flimbotzik scale—"

"Spare me the theology, please," Iversen begged. "Once a greech, always a greech, I say. And I can't help thinking that somehow, somewhere, Harkaway has committed some horrible error."

"Humanity is frail, fumbling, futile," Dr. Smullyan declared, coming upon them so suddenly that both officers jumped. "To err is human, to forgive divine, and I am an atheist, thank God!"

"That *mk'oog* is powerful stuff," the first officer said. "Or so they tell me," he added.

"This is more than mere *mk'oog*," Iversen said sourly. "Smullyan has been too long in space. It hits everyone in the long run—some sooner than others."

"Captain," the doctor said, ignoring these remarks as he ignored everything not on a cosmic level, which included the crew's ailments, "I am in full agreement with you. Young Harkaway has doomed that pretty little planet—"

"Moon," the first officer corrected. "It's a satellite, not a—"

"We ourselves were doomed *ab origine*, but the tragic flaw inherent in each one of our pitiful species is contagious, dooming all with whom we come in contact. And Harkaway is the most infectious carrier on the ship. Woe, I tell you. Woe!" And, with a hollow moan, the doctor left them to meditate upon the state of their souls, while he went off to his secret stores of oblivion.

"Wonder where he's hidden that *mk'oog*," Iversen brooded. "I've turned the ship inside out and I haven't been able to locate it."

The first officer shivered. "Somehow, although I know Smullyan's part drunk, part mad, he makes me a little nervous. He's been right so often on all the other voyages."

"Ruchbah!" Iversen said, not particularly grateful for support from such a dithyrambic source as the ship's medical officer. "Anyone who prophesies doom has a hundred per cent chance of ultimately being right, if only because of entropy."

He was still brooding over the first officer's thrust, even though he had been well aware that most of his officers and men considered him a sorehead for doubting Harkaway in the young man's moment of triumph. However, Iversen could not believe that Harkaway had undergone such a radical transformation. Even on the basis of *mpoola*, one obviously had to die before passing on to the next existence and Harkaway had been continuously alive—from the neck down, at least.

Furthermore, all that aside, Iversen just couldn't see Harkaway going on to a higher plane. Although he supposed the young man was well-meaning enough—he'd grant him that negligible virtue—wouldn't it be terrible to have a system of existence in which one was advanced on the basis of intent rather than result? The higher life-forms would degenerate into primitivism.

But weren't the Flimbotzik virtually primitive? Or so Harkaway had said, for Iversen himself had not had enough contact with them to determine their degree of sophistication, and only the spaceships gave Harkaway's claim the lie.

*

Iversen condescended to take a look at the opening chapter of Harkaway's book, just to see what the whole thing was about. The book began:

EVELYN E. SMITH

"What is the difference between life and death? Can we say definitely and definitively that life is life and death is death? Are we sure that death is not life and life is not death?

"No, we are not sure!

"Must the individuality have a corporeal essence in which to enshroud itself before it can proceed in its rapt, inexorable progress toward the Ultimate Non-actuality? And even if such be needful, why must the personal essence be trammeled by the same old worn-out habiliments of error?

"Think upon this!

"What is the extremest intensification of individuality? It is the All-encompassing Nothingness. Of what value are the fur, the feathers, the skin, the temporal trappings of imperfection in our perpetual struggle toward the final undefinable resolution into the Infinite Interplay of Cosmic Forces?

"Less than nothing!"

At this point, Iversen stopped reading and returned the manuscript to its creator, without a word. This last was less out of self-restraint than through sheer semantic inadequacy.

The young man might have spent his time more profitably in a little research on the biology or social organization of the Flimbotzik, Iversen thought bitterly when he had calmed down, thus saving the next expedition some work. But, instead, he'd been blinded by the flashy theological aspects of the culture and, as a result, the whole crew had gone metempsychotic.

This was going to be one of the *Herringbone's* more unendurable voyages, Iversen knew. And he couldn't put his foot down effectively, either, because the crew, all being gentlemen of independent means now, were outrageously independent.

21

ONCE A GREECH

However, in spite of knowing that all of them fully deserved what they got, Iversen couldn't help feeling guilty as he ate steak while the other officers consumed fish, vegetables and eggs in an aura of unbearable virtue.

"But if the soul transmigrates and not the body," he argued, "what harm is there in consuming the vacated receptacle?"

"For all you know," the first officer said, averting his eyes from Iversen's plate with a little—wholly gratuitous, to the captain's mind—shudder, "that cow might have housed the psyche of your grandmother."

"Well, then, by indirectly participating in that animal's slaughter, I have released my grandmother from her physical bondage to advance to the next plane. That is, if she was a good cow."

"You just don't understand," Harkaway said. "Not that you could be expected to."

"He's a clod," the radio operator agreed. "Forgive me, sir," he apologized as Iversen turned to glare incredulously at him, "but, according to mpoola, candor is a Step Upward."

"Onward and Upward," Harkaway commented, and Iversen was almost sure that, had he not been there, the men would have bowed their heads in contemplation, if not actual prayer.

*

As time went on, the greech thrived and grew remarkably stout on the Earth viands, which it consumed in almost improbable quantities. Then, one day, it disappeared and its happy squeal was heard no longer.

There was much mourning aboard the Herringbone—for, with its lovable personality and innocently engaging ways, the little fellow had won its way into the hearts of all the spacemen—until the first officer discovered a substantial pink cocoon resting on the ship's control board and rushed to the intercom to spread the glad tidings. That was a breach of regulations, of course, but Iversen knew when not to crowd his fragile authority.

"I should have known there was some material basis for the spiritual doctrine of *mpoola*," Harkaway declared with tears in his eyes as he regarded the dormant form of his little pet. "Was it not the transformation of the caterpillar into the butterfly that first showed us on Earth how the soul might emerge winged and beautiful from its vile house of clay? Gentlemen," he said, in a voice choked with emotion, "our little greech is about to become a zkoort. Praised be the Impersonal Being who has allowed such a miracle to take place before our very eyes. *J'goona lo mpoona*."

"Amen," said the first officer reverently.

All those in the control room bowed their heads except Iversen. And even he didn't quite have the nerve to tell them that the cocoon was pushing the *Herringbone* two points off course.

*

"Take that thing away before I lose my temper and clobber it," Iversen said impatiently as the zkoort dived low to buzz him, then whizzed just out of its reach on its huge, brilliant wings, giggling raucously.

"He was just having his bit of fun," the first officer said with reproach. "Have you no tolerance, Captain, no appreciation of the joys of golden youth?"

"A spaceship is no place for a butterfly," Iversen said, "especially a four-foot butterfly."

"How can you say that?" Harkaway retorted. "The *Herringbone* is the only spaceship that ever had one, to my knowledge. And I think I can safely say our lives are all a bit brighter and better and *m'poo'p* for having a zkoort among us. Thanks be to the Divine Nonentity for—"

ONCE A GREECH

"Poor little butterfly," Dr. Smullyan declared sonorously, "living out his brief life span so far from the fresh air, the sunshine, the pretty flowers—"

"Oh, I don't know that it's as bad as all that," the first officer said. "He hangs around hydroponics a lot and he gets a daily ration of vitamins." Then he paled. "But that's right—a butterfly does live only a day, doesn't it?"

"It's different with a zkoort," Harkaway maintained stoutly, though he also, Iversen noted, lost his ruddy color. "After all, he isn't really a butterfly, merely an analogous life-form."

"My, my! In four weeks, you've mastered their entomology as well as their theology and language," Iversen jeered. "Is there no end to your accomplishments, Lieutenant?"

Harkaway's color came back twofold. "He's already been around half a *thubb*," he pointed out. "Over two weeks."

"Well, the thing *is* bigger than a Terrestrial butterfly," Iversen conceded, "so you have to make some allowances for size. On the other hand—"

Laughing madly, the zkoort swooped down on him. Iversen beat it away with a snarl.

"Playful little fellow, isn't he?" the first officer said, with thoroughly annoying fondness.

"He likes you, Skipper," Harkaway explained. "*Urg'h n gurg'h*—or, to give it the crude Terran equivalent, living is loving. He can tell that beneath that grizzled and seemingly harsh exterior of yours, Captain—"

But, with a scream of rage, Iversen had locked himself into his cabin. Outside, he could hear the zkoort beating its wings against the door and wailing disappointedly.

*

Some days later, a pair of rapidly dulling wings were found on the floor of the hydroponics chamber. But of the zkoort's little body, there was no sign. An air of gloom and despondency hung over the *Herringbone* and even Iversen felt a pang, though he would never admit it without brainwashing.

During the next week, the men, seeking to forget their loss, plunged themselves into *mpoola* with real fanaticism. Harkaway took to wearing some sort of ecclesiastical robes which he whipped up out of the recreation room curtains. Iversen had neither the heart nor the courage to stop him, though this, too, was against regulations. Everyone except Iversen gave up eating fish and eggs in addition to meat.

Then, suddenly, one day a roly-poly blue animal appeared at the officers mess, claiming everyone as an old friend with loud squeals of joy. This time, Iversen was the only one who was glad to see him—really glad.

"Aren't you happy to see your little friend again, Harkaway?" he asked, scratching the delighted animal between the ears.

"Why, sure," Harkaway said, putting his fork down and leaving his vegetable *macédoine* virtually untasted. "Sure. I'm very happy—" his voice broke—"very happy."

"Of course, it does kind of knock your theory of the transmigration of souls into a cocked hat," the captain grinned. "Because, in order for the soul to transmigrate, the previous body's got to be dead, and I'm afraid our little pal here was alive all the time."

"Looks it, doesn't it?" muttered Harkaway.

"I rather think," Iversen went on, tickling the creature under the chin until it squealed happily, "that you didn't *quite* get the nuances of the language, did you, Harkaway? Because I gather now that the whole difficulty was a semantic one. The Flimbotzik were explaining the zoology of the native life-forms to you and you misunderstood it as their theology."

"Looks it, doesn't it?" Harkaway repeated glumly. "It certainly looks it."

"Cheer up," Iversen said, reaching over to slap the young man on the back—a bit to his own amazement. "No real harm done. What if the Flimbotzik are less primitive than you fancied? It makes our discovery the more worthwhile, doesn't it?"

At this point, the radio operator almost sobbingly asked to be excused from the table. Following his departure, there was a long silence. It was hard, Iversen realized in a burst of uncharacteristic tolerance, to have one's belief, even so newly born a credo, annihilated with such suddenness.

"After all, you did run across the Flimbotzik first," he told Harkaway as he spread gooseberry jam on a hard roll for the ravenous ex-zkoort (now a chu-wugg, he had been told). "That's the main thing, and a life-form that passes through two such striking metamorphoses is not unfraught with interest. You shall receive full credit, my boy, and your little mistake doesn't mean a thing except—"

"Doom," said Dr. Smullyan, sopping up the last of his gravy with a piece of bread. "Doom, doom, doom." He stuffed the bread into his mouth.

"Look, Smullyan," Iversen told him jovially, "you better watch out. If you keep talking that way, next voyage out we'll sign on a parrot instead of a medical officer. Cheaper and just as efficient."

Only the chu-wugg joined in his laughter.

"Ever since I can remember," the first officer said, looking gloomily at the doctor, "he's never been wrong. Maybe *he* has powers beyond our comprehension. Perhaps we sought at the end of the Galaxy what was in our own back yard all the time."

"Who was seeking what?" Iversen asked as all the officers looked at Smullyan with respectful awe. "I demand an answer!"

But the only one who spoke was the doctor. "Only Man is vile," he said, as if to himself, and fell asleep with his head on the table.

"Make a cult out of Smullyan," Iversen warned the others, "and I'll scuttle the ship!"

Later on, the first officer got the captain alone. "Look here, sir," he began tensely, "have you read Harkaway's book about *mpoola*?"

"I read part of the first chapter," Iversen told him, "and that was enough. Maybe to Harkaway it's eschatology, but to me it's just plain scatology!"

"But—"

"Why in Zubeneschamali," Iversen said patiently, "should I waste my time reading a book devoted to a theory which has already been proved erroneous? Answer me that!"

"I think you should have a look at the whole thing," the first officer persisted.

"Baham!" Iversen replied, but amiably enough, for he was in rare good humor these days. And he needed good humor to tolerate the way his officers and men were behaving. All right, they had made idiots of themselves; that was understandable, expected, familiar. But it wasn't the chu-wugg's fault. Iversen had never seen such a bunch of soreheads. Why did they have to take their embarrassment and humiliation out on an innocent little animal?

For, although no one actually mistreated the chu-wugg, the men avoided him as much as possible. Often Iversen would come upon the little fellow weeping from loneliness in a corner with no one to play with and, giving in to his own human weakness, the captain would dry the creature's tears and comfort him. In return, the chu-wugg would laugh at all his jokes, for he seemed to have acquired an elementary knowledge of Terran.

*

"By Vindemiatrix, Lieutenant," the captain roared as Harkaway, foiled in his attempt to scurry off unobserved, stood quivering before him, "why have you been avoiding me like this?"

"I didn't think I was avoiding you any particular way, sir," Harkaway said. "I mean does it appear like that, sir? It's only that I've been busy with my duties, sir."

"I don't know what's the matter with you! I told you I handsomely forgave you for your mistake."

"But I can never forgive myself, sir—"

"Are you trying to go over my head?" Iversen thundered.

"No, sir. I—"

"If I am willing to forgive you, you will forgive yourself. That's an order!"

"Yes, sir," the young man said feebly.

Harkaway had changed back to his uniform, Iversen noted, but he looked unkempt, ill, harrowed. The boy had really been suffering for his precipitance. Perhaps the captain himself had been a little hard on him.

Iversen modulated his tone to active friendliness. "Thought you might like to know the chu-wugg turned into a hoop-snake this morning!"

But Harkaway did not seem cheered by this social note. "So soon!"

"You knew there would be a fourth metamorphosis!" Iversen was disappointed. But he realized that Harkaway was bound to have acquired such fundamental data, no matter how he interpreted them. It was possible, Iversen thought, that the book could actually have some value, if there were some way of weeding fact from fancy, and surely there must be scholars trained in such an art, for Earth had many wholly indigenous texts of like nature.

"He's a thor'glitch now," Harkaway told him dully.

"And what comes next? . . . No, don't tell me. It's more fun not knowing beforehand. You know," Iversen went on, almost rubbing his hands together, "I think this species is going to excite more interest on Earth than the Flimbotzik themselves. After all, people are people, even if they're green, but an animal that changes shape so many times and so radically is really going to set biologists by the ears. What did you say the name of the species as a whole was?"

"I—I couldn't say, sir."

"Ah," Iversen remarked waggishly, "so there are one or two things you don't know about Flimbot, eh?"

Harkaway opened his mouth, but only a faint bleating sound came out.

*

As the days went on, Iversen found himself growing fonder and fonder of the thor'glitch. Finally, in spite of the fact that it had now attained the dimensions of a well-developed boa constrictor, he took it to live in his quarters.

Many was the quiet evening they spent together, Iversen entering acid comments upon the crew in the ship's log, while the thor'glitch looked over viewtapes from the ship's library.

The captain was surprised to find how much he—well, enjoyed this domestic tranquility. I must be growing old, he thought—old and mellow. And he named the creature Bridey, after a twentieth-century figure who had, he believed, been connected with another metempsychotic furor.

When the thor'glitch grew listless and began to swell in the middle, Iversen got alarmed and sent for Dr. Smullyan.

"Aha!" the medical officer declaimed, with a casual glance at the suffering snake. "The day of reckoning is at hand! Reap the fruit of your transgression, scurvy humans! Calamity approaches with jets aflame!"

Iversen clutched the doctor's sleeve. "Is he—is he going to die?"

"Unhand me, presumptuous navigator!" Dr. Smullyan shook the captain's fingers off his arm. "I didn't say he was going to die," he offered in ordinary bedside tones. "Not being a specialist in this particular sector, I am not qualified to offer an opinion, but, strictly off the record, I would hazard the guess that he's about to metamorphose again."

"He never did it in public before," Iversen said worriedly.

"The old order changeth," Smullyan told him. "You'd better call Harkaway."

"What does *he* know!"

"Too little and, at the same time, too much," the doctor declaimed, dissociating himself professionally from the case. "Too much and too little. Eat, drink, be merry, iniquitous Earthmen, for you died yesterday!"

"Oh, shut up," Iversen said automatically, and dispatched a message to Harkaway with the information that the thor'glitch appeared to be metamorphosing again and that his presence was requested in the captain's cabin.

The rest of the officers accompanied Harkaway, all of them with the air of attending a funeral rather than a rebirth, Iversen noted nervously. They weren't armed, though, so Bridey couldn't be turning into anything dangerous.

*

Now it came to pass that the thor'glitch's mid-section, having swelled to unbearable proportions, began to quiver. Suddenly, the skin split lengthwise and dropped cleanly to either side, like a banana peel.

Iversen pressed forward to see what fresh life-form the bulging cavity had held. The other officers all stood in a somber row without moving, for all along, Iversen realized, they had known what to expect, what was to come. And they had not told him. But then, he knew, it was his own fault; he had refused to be told.

Now, looking down at the new life-form, he saw for himself what it was. Lying languidly in the thor'glitch skin was a slender youth of a pallor which seemed excessive even for a member of a green-skinned race. He had large limpid eyes and a smile of ineffable sweetness.

"By Nopus Secundus," Iversen groaned. "I'm sunk."

"Naturally the ultimate incarnation for a life-form would be humanoid," Harkaway said with deep reproach. "What else?"

"I'm surprised you didn't figure that out for yourself, sir," the first officer added. "Even if you did refuse to read Harkaway's book, it seems obvious."

"Does it?" Smullyan challenged. "Does it, indeed? Is Man the highest form of life in an irrational cosmos? Then all causes are lost ones! . . . So many worlds," he muttered in more subdued tones, "so much to do, so little done, such things to be!"

"The Flimbotzik were telling Harkaway about their *own* life cycle," Iversen whispered as revelation bathed him in its murky light. "The human embryo undergoes a series of changes *inside* the womb. It's just that the Flimbotzik fetus develops *outside* the womb."

"Handily bypassing the earliest and most unpleasant stages of humanity," Smullyan sighed. "Oh, idyllic planet, where one need never be a child—where one need never see a child!"

"Then they were trying to explain their biology to you quite clearly and coherently, you lunkhead," Iversen roared at Harkaway, "and you took it for a religious doctrine!"

"Yes, sir," Harkaway said weakly. "I—I kind of figured that out myself in these last few weeks of intensive soul-searching. I—I'm sorry, sir. All I can say is that it was an honest mistake."

"Why, they weren't necessarily pet-lovers at all. Those animals they had with them were. . . . By Nair al Zaurak!" The captain's voice rose to a shriek as the whole enormity of the situation finally dawned upon him. "You went and kidnaped one of the children!"

"That's a serious charge, kidnaping," the first officer said with melancholy pleasure. "And you, as head of this expedition, Captain, are responsible. Ironic, isn't it?"

"Told you all this spelled doom and disaster," the doctor observed cheerfully.

Just then, the young humanoid sat up—with considerable effort, Iversen was disturbed to notice. But perhaps that was one of the consequences of being born. A new-born infant was weak; why not a new-born adult, then?

"Why doom?" the humanoid asked in a high, clear voice. "Why disaster?"

"You—you speak Terran?" the captain stammered.

Bridey gave his sad, sweet smile. "I was reared amongst you. You are my people. Why should I not speak your tongue?"

"But we're not your people," Iversen blurted, thinking perhaps the youth did not remember back to his greechi days. "We're an entirely different species—"

"Our souls vibrate in unison and that is the vital essence. But do not be afraid, shipmates; the Flimbotzik do not regard the abduction of a transitory corporeal shelter as a matter of any great moment.

Moreover, what took place could not rightly be termed abduction, for I came with you of my own volition—and the Flimbotzik recognize individual responsibility from the very first moment of the psyche's drawing breath in any material casing."

Bridey talked so much like Harkaway's book that Iversen was almost relieved when, a few hours later, the alien died. Of course the captain was worried about possible repercussions from the governments of both Terra and Flimbot, in spite of Bridey's assurances.

And he could not help but feel a pang when the young humanoid expired in his arms, murmuring, "Do not grieve for me, soul-mates. In the midst of life, there is life. . . . "

"Funny," Smullyan said, with one of his disconcerting returns to a professional manner, "all the other forms seemed perfectly healthy. Why did this one go like that? Almost as if he *wanted* to die."

"He was too good for this ship, that's what," the radio operator said, glaring at the captain. "Too fine and brave and—and noble."

"Yes," Harkaway agreed. "What truly sensitive soul could exist in a stultifying atmosphere like this?"

All the officers glared at the captain. He glared back with right good will. "How come you gentlemen are still with us?" he inquired. "One would have thought you would have perished of pure sensibility long since, then."

"It's not nice to talk that way," the chief petty officer burst out, "not with him lying there not yet cold. . . . Ah," he heaved a long sigh, "we'll never see his like again."

"Ay, that we won't," agreed the crew, huddled in the corridor outside the captain's cabin.

Iversen sincerely hoped not, but he forbore to speak.

*

ONCE A GREECH

Since Bridey had reached the ultimate point in his life cycle, it seemed certain that he was not going to change into anything else and so he was given a spaceman's burial. Feeling like a put-upon fool, Captain Iversen read a short prayer as Bridey's slight body was consigned to the vast emptiness of space.

Then the airlock clanged shut behind the last mortal remains of the ill-fated extraterrestrial and that was the end of it.

But the funereal atmosphere did not diminish as the ship forged on toward Earth. Gloomy days passed, one after the other, during which no one spoke, save to issue or dispute an order. Looking at himself one day in the mirror on his cabin wall, the captain realized that he was getting old. Perhaps he ought to retire instead of still dreaming of a new command and a new crew.

And then one day, as he sat in his cabin reading the Spaceman's Credo, the lights on the *Herringbone* went out, all at once, while the constant hum of the motors died down slowly, leaving a strange, uncomfortable silence. Iversen found himself suspended weightless in the dark, for the gravity, of course, had gone off with the power. What, he wondered, had come to pass? He often found himself thinking in such terms these days.

Hoarse cries issued from the passageway outside; then he heard a squeak as his cabin door opened and persons unknown floated inside, breathing heavily.

"The power has failed, sir!" gasped the first officer's voice.

"That has not escaped my notice," Iversen said icily. Were not even his last moments to be free from persecution?

"It's all that maniac Smullyan's fault. He stored his *mk'oog* in the fuel tanks. After emptying them out first, that is. We're out of fuel."

34

EVELYN E. SMITH

The captain put a finger in his book to mark his place, which was, he knew with a kind of supernal detachment, rather foolish, because there was no prospect of there ever being lights to read by again.

"Put him in irons, if you can find him," he ordered. "And tell the men to prepare themselves gracefully for a lingering death."

Iversen could hear a faint creak as the first officer drew himself to attention in the darkness. "The men of the *Herringbone*, sir," he said, stiffly, "are always prepared for calamity."

"Ay, that we are," agreed various voices.

So they were all there, were they? Well, it was too much to expect that they would leave him in death any more than they had in life.

"It is well," Iversen said. "It is well," he repeated, unable to think of anything more fitting.

Suddenly the lights went on again and the ship gave a leap. From his sprawling position on the floor, amid his recumbent officers, Iversen could hear the hum of motors galvanized into life.

"But if the fuel tanks are empty," he asked of no one in particular, "where did the power come from?"

"I am the power," said a vast, deep voice that filled the ship from hold to hold.

"And the glory," said the radio operator reverently. "Don't forget the glory."

"No," the voice replied and it was the voice of Bridey, resonant with all the amplitude of the immense chest cavity he had acquired. "Not the glory, merely the power. I have reached a higher plane of existence. I am a spaceship."

"Praise be to the Ultimate Nothingness!" Harkaway cried.

"Ultimate Nothingness, nothing!" Bridey said impatiently. "I achieved it all myself."

ONCE A GREECH

"Then that's how the Flimbotzi spaceships were powered!" Iversen exclaimed. "By themselves—the Flimbotzik themselves, I mean—"

"Even so," Bridey replied grandly. "And this lofty form of life happens to be one which we poor humans cannot reach unassisted. Someone has to build the shell for us to occupy, which is the reason humans dwell together in fellowship and harmony—"

"You purposely got Harkaway to take you aboard the *Herringbone*," Iversen interrupted wrathfully. "You—you stowaway!"

Bridey's laugh rang through the ship, setting the loose parts quivering. "Of course. When first I set eyes upon this vessel of yours, I saw before me the epitome of all dreams. Never had any of our kind so splendid an encasement. And, upon determining that the vessel was, as yet, a soulless thing, I got myself aboard; I was born, I died, and was reborn again with the greatest swiftness consonant with comfort, so that I could awaken in this magnificent form. Oh, joy, joy, joy!"

"You know," Iversen said, "now that I hear one of you talk at length, I really can't blame Harkaway for his typically imbecilic mistake."

"We are a wordy species," Bridey conceded.

"You had no right to do what you did," Iversen told him, "no right to take over—"

"But I didn't take over," Bridey the *Herringbone* said complacently. "I merely remained quiescent and content in the knowledge of my power until yours failed. Without me, you would even now be spinning in the vasty voids, a chrome-trimmed sepulcher. Now, three times as swiftly as before, shall I bear you back to the planet you very naively call home."

"Not three times as fast, please!" Iversen was quick to plead. "The ship isn't built—*we're* not built to stand such speeds."

36

The ship sighed. "Disappointment needs must come to all—the high, the low, the man, the spaceship. It must be borne—" the voice broke—"bravely. Somehow."

"What am I going to do?" Iversen asked, turning to the first officer for advice for the first time ever. "I was planning to ask for a transfer or resign my command when we got back to Earth. But how can I leave Bridey in the hands of the IEE(E)?"

"You can't, sir," the first officer said. "Neither can we."

"If you explain," Harkaway offered timidly, "perhaps they'll present the ship to the government."

Both Iversen and the first officer snorted, united for once. "Not the IEE(E)," Iversen said. "They'd—they'd exhibit it or something and charge admission."

"Oh, no," Bridey cried, "I don't want to be exhibited! I want to sail through the trackless paths of space. What good is a body like this if I cannot use it to its fullest?"

"Have no fear," Iversen assured it. "We'll just—" he shrugged, his dreams of escape forever blighted—"just have to buy the ship from the IEE(E), that's all."

"Right you are, sir," the first officer agreed. "We must club together, every man Jack of us, and buy her. Him. It. That's the only decent thing to do."

"Perhaps they won't sell," Harkaway worried. "Maybe—"

"Oh, they'll sell, all right," Iversen said wearily. "They'd sell the chairman of the board, if you made them an offer, and throw in all the directors if the price was right."

"And then what will we do?" the first officer asked. "Once the ship has been purchased, what will our course be? What, in other words, are we to do?"

ONCE A GREECH

It was Bridey who answered. "We will speed through space seeking, learning, searching, until you—all of you—pass on to higher planes and, leaving the frail shells you now inhabit, occupy proud, splendid vessels like the one I wear now. Then, a vast transcendent flotilla, we will seek other universes. . . . "

"But we don't become spaceships," Iversen said unhappily. "We don't become anything."

"How do you know we don't?" Smullyan demanded, appearing on the threshold. "How do you know what we become? Build thee more stately spaceships, O my soul!"

Above all else, Iversen was a space officer and dereliction of duty could not be condoned even in exceptional circumstances. "Put him in irons, somebody!"

"Ask Bridey why there were only forty-five spaceships on his planet!" the doctor yelled over his shoulder as he was dragged off. "Ask where the others went—where they are now."

But Bridey wouldn't answer that question.